MOIRA MILLER

Where Does Andy Go?

Illustrated by Doreen Caldwell

D1514457

A Magnet Book

First published 1985
by Methuen Children's Books Ltd
This Magnet edition published 1987
by Methuen Children's Books Ltd
11 New Fetter Lane, London EC4P 4EE
Text copyright © 1985 Moira Miller
Illustrations copyright © 1985 Doreen Caldwell
Printed in Great Britain
by Richard Clay Ltd, Bungay, Suffolk

ISBN 0 416 00562 4

Contents

1
The day the holiday was decided

This is Andy.

Andy has a sister called Tivvy and a brother called Dave. They are both bigger than him, and they're allowed to go out on the road on their bikes. Andy can ride his on the pavement.

Andy's little brother, Todger, goes to Playgroup – and then there's Rosie, the baby. Todger and Rosie play in the garden.

Andy goes right in the middle of the family, between Tivvy and Dave who are big, and Todger and Rosie who are small.

One Sunday afternoon, towards the end of the winter, everyone was trying to decide where they should go for a summer holiday. Everyone except Rosie, who was too little to remember what a summer holiday was.

'Camping again?' said Dad. Everyone groaned.

'Remember last time, when all the cows walked through our picnic and I tripped over the string and the tent fell down?' said Andy. He crawled around the floor, mooing. Todger started to cry.

'Don't like cows,' he hiccuped.

'Never again!' said Mum. 'How about another holiday with Auntie Jane?'

'She went barmy when I played football in the front garden,' said Dave gloomily. 'And remember when Todger dug up the flowers?'

'Maybe not,' said Mum and she sighed. 'All I really want to do is sit in the sunshine, somewhere peaceful.'

'With lots of long walks and some fishing,' said Dad.

'Pop music and shops,' said Tivvy, bouncing up and down with her eyes shut. She was listening to a tape on her small cassette player with the earphones.

'Somewhere I can play football and swim,' said Dave.

'How about you, Andy?' asked Dad. 'What would you like to do?'

'Don't know,' said Andy shrugging. 'Something different.'

'Great!' said Dad. 'That's a big help.'

Later, when Uncle Billy popped in at teatime, Andy climbed up on the kitchen stool beside him.

'Where do you think we ought to go?' he said.

'Treasure Island,' said Uncle Billy. 'Lots of free beer and pirates. Ha, ha!' He hopped round the kitchen on one leg with the tea cosy perched on his shoulder, pretending it was a parrot. Andy nearly fell off the stool giggling.

'Pack it in!' said Mum, grabbing the cosy as he hopped past. 'This is serious.'

So Uncle Billy packed it in, had a mug of tea, and thought about it.

'Leave it with me,' he said. 'I'll have a PONDER.'

Early the next Saturday morning, Dad stuck his nose out of the door and sniffed. It was still too cold and wet to start digging the garden. He was just going back to pour another mug of tea when an ancient blue van rattled round the corner.

It was Uncle Billy from the garage.

'Roll up, roll up!' he shouted, leaning out of the van. 'Come and join the Magical Mystery Holiday Tour.' Everyone raced out to meet him.

'Where to?' said Mum.

'End of the Rainbow,' laughed Uncle Billy, bundling Tivvy, Dave, Andy and Todger into the back of the van. Dad lifted Rosie's carrycot in beside them, climbed in the front with Mum and off they rattled into the High Street traffic.

They bounced along by the canal bank, where the water was grey and dirty, spotted with little rings of raindrops.

'Roll on summer,' said Dad, shivering and zipping up his anorak.

They clattered past the old empty factories on the edge of town and out into the country where the brown earth lay cold and muddy and the trees were still bare.

Here and there under the hedges there was still a little patch of snow and in the corner of a field a tiny white lamb with legs like wobbly pipe cleaners nuzzled up to a fat grey sheep.

'Want a biscuit,' grumbled Todger.

'Not long now,' called Uncle Billy. 'George'll have the kettle on.'

'Who's George?' they all shouted, but Uncle Billy just smiled.

They turned off the main road at last and bounced into a muddy yard between a small stone cottage and an old barn. Tivvy, Dave, Andy and Todger tumbled over each other, pushing and shoving, out into the yard.

A little round, crinkly, brown face with a mop of fluffy white hair popped up at a window in the barn and then vanished again.

'Right, George!' shouted Uncle Billy, grabbing Todger before he sat in a muddy puddle. 'Here they are. Do you think you can help?'

The little old man with the crinkly brown face came round the corner of the barn and stood smiling at them. He was not much bigger than Tivvy. When he

11

smiled there were spaces where most of his teeth should have been. Andy had spaces, too, at the front where his new teeth were growing in, but not nearly so many.

'Got just the ticket, right here,' he said and led them round to a small side door in the barn.

'I'm not spending a holiday in *there*!' sniffed Mum, bouncing after him. Uncle Billy winked at Dad and they all followed Mum into the high, dark shed.

'Here we are,' said George proudly. 'She's me pride and joy.'

Standing behind Dad in the gloom, Andy could just make out a tall square shape with huge tyres and mudguards.

George felt his way to the front of the barn, tripping over empty paint pots. Somewhere a cat squawked and shot past them out of the side door.

''Aint she a beauty?' said George. With a crash he pushed open the huge doors at the front of the barn and the watery winter sunlight fell on two polished silver headlamps, shining like full moons, and a dusty windscreen.

Everyone stood and stared in amazement.

'It's a bus,' said Dad at last. 'What on earth's it doing here?'

'A real double decker,' squeaked Mum. 'And look what's happened to it!'

It was a real double decker, but like no other bus any of them had ever seen before. From top to bottom it was painted all over in a great splash of different colours.

Over the bright, shiny blue roof, white-painted puffy clouds spread out and down the sides. A painted rainbow reached up one side of the bus, across the top and right down the other side. All around the bottom, under the downstairs windows, painted green grass was covered with brilliantly coloured flowers, rabbits and birds.

They walked round slowly, staring at the pictures and colours. On the back of the bus, Andy found a bright blue painted duck pond with four fat white ducks.

And at all the windows, upstairs and down, there were curtains. Flowered curtains, striped curtains, checked curtains, all different colours and patterns, and all closed. There never was a bus quite like it.

Mum stood and stared.

'It's magic,' whispered Andy.

'Can we go in?' said Dad, Dave and Tivvy together.

George opened the door by the driver's seat, and there was another surprise. Inside, the bus was fitted out just like a little house. All the seats had been taken out, except the benches up at the back which stood round three sides of a table. Along one side were a small cooker and sink with cupboards underneath. Along the other side ran a low bench with soft cushions.

'I don't believe this,' said Dad, shaking his head and opening and closing cupboards.

'It's gorgeous,' said Mum, bouncing on the soft cushions and pulling open the curtains. 'I love your carpets!'

The floor was covered with a strange collection of rugs. Like the curtains they were all different patterns and colours.

There were lots of questions after that.

'Where did you get it?'

'Does it really go?'

'Can you sleep in it?'

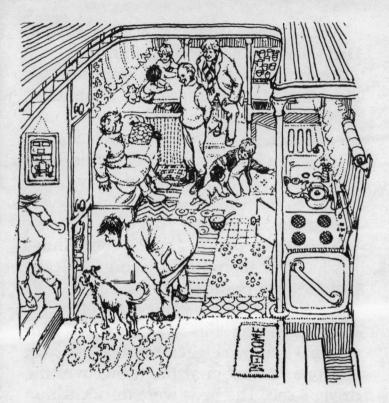

George smiled his huge toothless grin. 'Used to be a bus driver,' he smiled, running his hand round the steering wheel. 'I missed them old dears when I retired so I bought this one and did it all up meself. It's meant for a holiday, but it's too big for me. Besides, I can't go this year – I've just bought another one.'

'Go on!' said Uncle Billy. 'You'll love it. I'll come with you and drive.'

Nobody said anything. Mum looked at Dad. Dad looked back at Mum.

'I suppose we could go anywhere we liked,' said Dad at last, a little doubtfully.

'And if we didn't like it we could move on somewhere else,' said Mum smiling.

'Or stay if you wanted,' said Uncle Billy.

'At the seaside!' shouted Tivvy and Dave.

'Sampies,' squealed Todger.

'On holiday on a *real* bus?' yelled Andy.

'Plenty of room,' said George. 'Sleeps two downstairs and the rest are up . . .' His voice was lost in the clatter of feet.

Upstairs, the bus was divided with curtains into two bigger rooms at the back and one tiny room at the front, over the driver's cab. The beds were thick cushion mattresses on the floor. Andy climbed round to look into the little front room.

'Mum and I'll sleep downstairs,' said Dad. 'Uncle Billy and Dave can have the bigger bedroom at the back there.'

'Andy, Todger and Rosie's carrycot in the middle room,' said Mum, 'and Tivvy up front.' Andy stuffed his hands deep in the pockets of his jeans and scowled.

'*Excuse* me!' said Tivvy in her Madam

voice, pushing past him. She lay down on the cushion bed and stretched out.

'It's too short,' she wailed. Her feet stuck right out at the end.

'And Dave won't fit,' said Dad. 'He's nearly as big as Tivvy. How about Todger then?' But Todger didn't like the idea of sleeping in a little room all on his own.

Andy looked up at Mum. She winked.

'Only one thing for it,' she said. *'That's* where Andy goes.'

'Tea's ready,' called George from the

bottom of the stairs. They all turned and clumped down again – except Andy.

He stood all alone in the tiny bedroom above the driver's cab. When the others had all gone back across the yard to the cottage he lay down and stretched out on the little bed that just fitted him.

'I'm going on holiday,' he whispered to the empty top deck. 'On a *real* bus!' Then he rolled over, curled up on the mattress and bounced with pure happiness.

2
The day the bus left

One afternoon in the last week before the summer holidays, Andy was wobbling along a low wall on his way home from school.

'We're going on holiday on a bus,' he shouted, swinging his bag round his head.

'So what!' said his pal, Steve. 'We're going on a plane – *and* we're staying in a hotel with a swimming pool.'

'I'm going to *live* on the bus,' said Andy, jumping down, 'with a bedroom upstairs.'

'Nobody lives on a bus!' shouted Steve. He grabbed Andy's bag and threw it into the garden.

'Well we are,' said Andy, reaching for the bag. A lady came to the window and knocked on the glass.

'We're leaving on Saturday morning,' he shouted as they raced off down the road. 'Come round and see if we don't.'

As he ran up his front path, he could still hear Steve shouting.

'Don't believe you, don't believe you. Nobody lives on a bus!'

At home, in the last week before the holidays, it was murder.

Mum always got into a real tizz about holidays. She washed and ironed everything she could lay her hands on. You only had to take off a tee-shirt or a pair of socks and they vanished into the washing machine, never to be seen again – until the holiday.

'No, you can't have your Superman tee-shirt,' she told Andy for the umpteenth time. 'It's all ready to pack. Wear an old one.'

By the end of the week, Andy had to go out to play in shorts and tee-shirts that were too small and should really have been handed on to Todger.

But Mum didn't notice. She was too busy writing holiday lists. She scribbled them on scraps of paper, old letters, advertisements for double glazing that popped through the letterbox – she even wrote a list on the edge of one of Tivvy's pop posters.

'Oh Mum!' wailed Tivvy, attacking the poster with a rubber. 'You're *hopeless*.'

'True,' said Mum. She was sorting through another pile of ironing and hadn't really been listening.

'Nuts!' said Tivvy, shaking her head.

'Too much packing,' said Dave. 'She's gone funny.'

But somehow, funny or not, Mum finally managed to get all the washing and ironing done, and make up a list of everything they would need to take on holiday. Dad and Uncle Billy took Tivvy, Dave and Andy to the Supermarket where they filled basket after basket with food.

'You've enough there to feed an army!' said old George, watching them load it all into the bus that evening. 'They'll never eat that lot.'

'Don't you believe it,' said Dad, helping Tivvy and the others to pack everything safely into cupboards and drawers.

By the time they went back home, Todger and Rosie were in bed. Mum had packed the last of the bags and had flopped into an armchair in front of the television.

There was something very exciting about that row of bags in the hall, Andy thought. Stuffed fat and full with the zips bulging, they sat in a neatly labelled row.

The big green tartan bag had a red ticket with MUM DAD AND ROSIE written on it. There was a neat, square, pink sports bag with TIVVY on the ticket, an old green sports bag with a label that said DAVE. You could tell it was Dave's anyway because his football boots made bumpy shapes in the side.

Andy had a big, orange duffel bag with a smiling yellow face on the side and a label saying ANDY hanging down in front of its nose. He peeked inside, and there right at the top was his Superman tee-shirt. The last bag was a little, fat, roly-poly brown one with TODGER on the label.

Andy was standing staring at them when Dad came through.

'What's up?' he said.

'The bags look a bit like us, don't they?' said Andy. 'Todger's roly-poly and Tivvy's always wearing pink things and . . .'

'You know, you're right,' Dad laughed. 'Just don't tell Mum she's a big fat tartan

bag! Come on, let's go and make her a cup of tea, and then bed.'

After supper Andy washed his face, brushed his teeth and climbed up into the top bunk. Beneath him, Todger was fast asleep.

'Night, night, sleep tight,' whispered Dad, tucking him in.

'Can't,' hissed Andy. 'My tummy's full of bubbles.' Dad poked him and he giggled.

Andy felt as if he would never be able to settle down that night. He wriggled and tossed and turned until the bed squeaked and his pillow ended up as a scrunched-up bundle. He must have nodded off at last though, for the next thing he knew, Mum was banging about in the kitchen. He knew it was her because she was singing a pop song very badly and making up nonsense words as she went along.

Andy climbed down out of bed, pulled on the clean clothes that were lying neatly folded on his chair and raced through to the kitchen.

'Breakfast!' sang Mum, banging the spoons together. 'Last chance for a boiled egg before the holiday.' But Andy was far too excited to eat much at all.

'When's Uncle Billy coming with the bus?' he asked, fidgeting on his chair.

'Soon,' said Mum, shovelling egg into Rosie.

'How soon?' he asked.

'Too soon,' said Dad, shoving both of Todger's feet into one leg of his dungarees. Todger squawked and they had to take them off and start again.

And then, at long last, Dave came rushing in from the front garden.

'He's here – he's here!' he yelled, dancing round the table. He grabbed his old sports bag and rushed out again, followed by all the family.

The bus looked beautiful. Bouncing slowly up the road with the sun gleaming on polished glass, the painted rainbow seemed brighter than ever. George had hung coloured balloons from the windows and Uncle Billy in the driver's seat wore one of his most brilliant shirts.

Parp-pa-parp-parp! he tooted. The lady at the end of the road hung out of her bedroom window in her dressing gown with her hair still bundled up in rollers.

'Well I never!' she said.

In less time than it took to say 'Happy Families', all the bags were loaded, Dad had locked the front door and Rosie's carrycot and push-chair were handed up into the bus. Andy and Todger climbed up on to the seats at the back, bubbling with excitement.

'Right, that's it,' said Mum. 'If I've forgotten anything, it's too late.' Uncle Billy started the engine – and at last they were off.

With a hooting and tooting, a laughing and singing, the big bright Rainbow Bus rolled down to the end of the road. The balloons bobbed as if waving goodbye. The neighbours cheered and waved back.

'The wheels on the bus go round and

round...' sang Uncle Billy and they all joined in. As they turned the corner into the High Street, a boy standing with his Mum outside the Supermarket turned to look.

'Bye, Steve,' yelled Andy, as loudly as he could. 'I'm going on holiday on a *real* bus!' He pressed his nose flat against the window and pulled a funny face. A red balloon drifted loose and floated high above the busy Saturday morning traffic. Steve stood and stared with his mouth

open as the bus rattled off down the road
with everybody singing.

'The passengers on the bus are off on holiday,
Off on holiday, off on holiday . . . . '

3
The night it rained

Everyone agreed that the Rainbow Bus was simply the best holiday idea ever.

'It's perfect,' said Dad. 'We can go just where we like, and when we find the right place we'll stop there.'

By the middle of the afternoon on the first day they were beginning to look for somewhere to spend the night.

'There's a poster on the tree by that farm gate,' Mum shouted. 'Eggs, Milk and Caravans.'

'Don't want any caravans, thank you,' said Uncle Billy, pulling up at the gate. 'Not that hungry.'

Mum knocked on the farmhouse door and four or five dogs tumbled out, barking and wagging their tails. They were followed by a tall lady in a flowery dress, green wellingtons and a man's cap. She smiled and pointed to a path that led through the trees at the back of the house. Mum turned and waved to the bus to follow, and set off to walk down the path.

'Hold on to your hats,' called Uncle Billy and the bus bumped and joggled down through the trees to a grassy clearing where a little river gurgled, brown and sparkling over smooth stones. Mum was lying in the long grass with her sandals beside her.

'Perfect,' she sighed. 'Just perfect.'

And so it was, thought Andy, stretching out that first night in his little bedroom above the driver's cab. All around him the bright evening sun still shone through the green and gold leaves, making shadow patterns on his sleeping bag. He lay and watched as the fields and hills across the river grew darker.

Somewhere among the treetops, an owl hooted as Tivvy and Dave tiptoed up the stairs to bed. Andy was fast asleep long before Uncle Billy came up to join them.

The days by the river stretched out long and lazy. Uncle Billy went exploring with Tivvy and Dave. Mum, Todger and Rosie picnicked by the river-bank while Dad and

Andy went fishing. They never caught anything, but Andy thought it was fun all the same.

He loved it best, though, in the early mornings before the others were awake. If he lay very quietly in his bed and listened he could hear the tiny scritch-scratch of the birds walking across the top of the bus. The treetops were full of them singing their breakfast songs. Most mornings the fields were hidden at first under a mist, like a soft quilt, and the bushes along the river-bank were covered in silvery cobwebs hanging with tiny wet beads of shining dew.

'The spiders have hung their washing out to dry,' whispered Mum on one of their very-early-morning walks. And that was exactly what it looked like.

It went on like that for days, with soft misty mornings and hot afternoons.

'Too hot for the fish,' said Dad, kicking off his rubber boots and paddling his toes in the water.

'Too hot for me,' said Uncle Billy, stretching out in the shade with Tivvy and Dave flopped beside him.

'Too hot for them,' said Mum as Todger and Rosie became more and more crotchety. 'Proper little hot cross buns.'

'What we all need are some sea breezes,' said Dad, as they sat outside the bus that night drinking their bedtime cocoa. 'I think we should move on tomorrow.'

'Yes!' they all agreed with a shout.

'Good idea,' said Mum. 'Do you think it's ever going to rain again?'

'We'll maybe get a little tonight,' said Uncle Billy, stretching and yawning. 'There's some cloud over the hills.'

But he was wrong. There was not just a little rain – there was an awful lot.

Andy heard it first. In the darkness of the middle of the night he was wakened by a brilliant flash of light, followed by a loud rumbling crash. He knelt on his bed and looked out. A wind danced and swooped among the trees around the bus and he jumped back as another flash lit up their tossing branches.

With the second clap of thunder, Todger sat up crying and in no time Tivvy, Dave and Uncle Billy were up too. A third flash was followed by the heaviest rain Andy had ever seen. It battered on the roof like drumsticks and ran down the sides of the bus in great dripping waterfalls.

'Shut the windows, quick!' yelled Tivvy, stumbling around and falling over the others in the dark. Downstairs, Mum and Dad were doing the same thing and Rosie was yelling even louder than the storm.

'Put the kettle on,' sighed Mum. 'Nobody's going to get much sleep in this.' The thunder came and went, sometimes it was far off, grumbling among the hills. At other times it crept up and crashed around the bus making them all jump. Todger crawled into Mum's sleeping bag and Tivvy sat and squealed with a cushion held over her head.

'There's an awful lot of water coming down from the hills,' said Dad, peering out into the dark. 'Hope the river doesn't flood.'

'Eeeeeeek!' screeched Mum. 'Rosie's push-chair! We're going to lose it. I left it down by the river.' Sure enough, in the light from the bus they could just see the shining silver handle of the little red push-chair sitting on the stones by the river-bank in the pouring rain. Already the rushing brown water was lapping up round the wheels.

'I'll get it,' yelled Dad, searching around for his clothes. Andy was sitting on his trousers and Tivvy had pulled on his socks to keep her feet warm.

'Hurry up!' shouted Mum. 'It's going!' Dad gave up trying to get dressed, pulled on his wellingtons and dashed out into the rain in his pyjamas.

'Look at that!' said Dave. 'It's floating away.'

'Be careful!' shouted Mum, as Dad waded out – but he was just too late.

The little red push-chair was swept off across the river and jammed under the branch of a tree on the far side.

'He'll never get over there,' said Uncle Billy. 'It's far too deep now.'

But Dad knew just what to do.

'Fishing rod, quickly,' he panted, squelching back up to the bus.

'You can't go fishing at this time of night!' squeaked Mum as he flapped past her, wet and dripping, to grab the rod. He raced back down to the river, swung back the rod and the line snaked out across the water.

'He's going to catch the pram,' shouted Andy, bouncing on the cushions. 'He's going to catch it!'

Dad missed on the first go – and the second.

'Oh no!' wailed Mum as he waded further out and the rain lashed down, heavier and heavier. Third time lucky. The line curled around the push-chair and caught. Dad pulled and heaved it, bobbing slowly towards him through the rushing water.

He flopped back into the bus at last, pyjamas soaked and boots full of water.

'My hero!' giggled Mum, pouring another mug of tea and handing him a towel. Tivvy peered out from underneath her cushion.

'We'll be cut off for days and days,' she wailed dramatically, 'and starve to death.'

'Rubbish,' said Dave. 'They'll send in a Rescue Helicopter and we'll get on the News on telly.' Dad laughed.

'You're both daft,' he said. 'The river

will have gone back down again by breakfast-time. And we're off to the seaside tomorrow. Remember?'

And so they were.

4
The day Todger got lost

It was fun at the seaside. Noisy and lively and jam-packed with people.

'Look at the shops!' squealed Tivvy as the bus trundled slowly along the prom. 'There's one with lots of tee-shirts and badges. Maybe I'll get some pop stickers there.'

'Sampies!' yelled Todger, jumping up and down on the cushions. He had just spotted the beach.

'And donkeys!' shouted Andy. 'I've never been on one. Can I have a go? Can I, Dad?'

Everyone wanted to do something different.

'What about you, Billy?' said Dad. 'What would you like to do?'

'Park this blooming bus,' grumbled

Uncle Billy. Every car park seemed to be packed full of cars and vans of all sorts of sizes and colours. The town was very, very busy.

They found a place at last in a car park with caravans at the end of the beach, and agreed that the only thing to do was for everyone to split up and then meet again at lunchtime. Tivvy and Dave were old enough to go to the shops on their own with their pocket money. Mum and Dad were taking Todger and Rosie down to the beach to dig sand-pies. That left Uncle Billy and Andy standing looking at each other.

'Right,' said Uncle Billy. 'You and me are going to find a donkey. But there's two things we need to do first.'

He took Andy's hand and led the way into a big shop that was bright with shining beach balls, rubber rings and buckets full of paper flags. Uncle Billy rummaged on a table at the back.

'Here we are,' he said. 'Can't be at the seaside without a topper!' He plonked a big red cowboy hat on Andy's head. Suddenly, everything went very dark.

'It's too big,' Andy giggled.

'You might grow into it,' laughed Uncle Billy, 'in about a hundred years.' They were fooling about, trying on more hats when the shop lady came up.

'Can I help you, sir?' she asked, giving Uncle Billy a funny look. He was wearing a shiny black and white checked bowler hat, tipped over to one side.

'Yes,' he said, admiring himself in a little round mirror. 'I'll have this one I think. How about you, Andy?'

But Andy couldn't make up his mind. The more he tried on, the harder it was. Uncle Billy found him soldiers' hats, straw hats, blue denim caps, a little round sailor's hat, even a shiny eye shade that made everything in the shop look green. They were none of them quite right.

Then Andy saw the one he wanted.

'Well . . . I don't know,' said the lady doubtfully. 'It's a bit crumpled. One of last year's, you see.'

Andy shoved the hat on his head. It was a bright blue cloth cap, the same colour as his shorts. But best of all it had a fat felt seagull with a huge yellow beak, perched on top. Andy shook his head and the seagull wobbled. They fell about laughing.

'Andy,' gasped Uncle Billy. 'You're even dafter than me!' They left the shop, still laughing, with the seagull nodding up and down and Andy running and skipping to try and keep up with Uncle Billy.

'What was the other thing?' he puffed. 'You said there were two things we needed.'

'A little something to keep us going,' said Uncle Billy, heading for an ice-cream

kiosk.

They sat on the sea wall, eating huge dripping cones and watched the people on the beach. It was crowded. Someone kicked a red and white ball which bounced off Uncle Billy, and a little dog ran up and down, barking. You could hardly see the sand for coloured towels and deck-chairs.

Andy had to wait ages in a queue for a ride on an old, grey, shaggy donkey.

'It doesn't go very fast,' he said, bouncing up and down and poking his heels into its warm furry sides. He held on tight, but the donkey plodded on, floof, floof, floof, through the soft sand at the same slow pace – like a big clockwork toy.

'I expect he's hungry,' said Uncle Billy. 'So'm I. It's time we met the others for lunch.'

But when they got to the Post Office where they had arranged to meet, there was only Mum standing with Rosie in the push-chair, and looking very hot and bothered.

'We've lost Todger,' she said. 'We were in Woolworth's. I just turned my back for a minute and he vanished. Dad's gone to look for him with Dave and Tivvy.' Then she smiled. 'I like your hat, Andy. Where on earth did you find one like that?'

'Chose it himself – don't blame me,' said Uncle Billy, patting the seagull. 'Come on, Andy, we'll go on a Todger hunt too. He can't be far away.'

They searched in and out of all the shops along the sea front. They met Dad and Tivvy and Dave, but none of them had seen Todger and the shops seemed busier than ever.

'There he is!' shouted Andy. He caught a glimpse through the crowd of a small boy in red dungarees with an untidy mop of brown curls. He was crying.

''Scuse me!' said Dad, shoving his way through. 'Where have you been then?'

A lady standing beside the small boy turned and stared at Dad.

'Oh, sorry,' he said. 'Thought he was ours. We've lost him.'

'You can have this one if you like!' snapped the lady, trying to wipe chocolate stains from the small boy's face and hands, and her dress.

'No thanks!' said Dad. They searched everywhere. In and out of all the shops and along the beach. Uncle Billy ran back to the bus to see if Todger was there, but there was no sign of him.

'I'm starving,' said Dave at last, flopping down on a bench.

'Me too,' said Andy, joining him. Mum didn't say anything. She just stood there looking more and more worried.

'Come on,' said Dad. 'This is no good, we'd better go to the Police Station. But stick together. Don't want anyone else to get lost.'

It was a long walk through the hot crowded streets. Rosie started to cry. Dad asked a couple of people the way, and at last they found the Police Station.

The front hall was cool and dark after the sun. Uncle Billy nudged Andy and pointed to the black and white shiny tiled floor in front of the desk.

'Just like my hat,' he said. But Andy didn't feel like laughing. Neither did anyone else.

The big sergeant behind the desk listened to Dad and wrote things down in a book.

'Lost a small boy?' he said. 'Name of Thomas Rodger.' Then he looked up and smiled.

'Is he a little terror – about so high – in red dungarees? Brown curly hair.'

'That's him,' said Mum. She was so excited she was nearly crying.

'Been here for ages,' said the police sergeant. 'Someone found him in Woolworth's. He's had an orange juice and at the moment he's having sausage, egg and chips in the canteen with one of our ladies.'

'Typical!' sniffed Tivvy, as they all piled

up the stairs to the canteen.

There, sure enough, sitting at a table with a lady in a police uniform fussing over him, was Todger. He was munching quietly through a big brown sausage.

Mum and Dad cuddled him. Mum cried a bit and Dad told him off for wandering away. Todger cried a bit and finished his sausage, egg and chips, and everyone else had a cup of tea.

'Funny little lad that,' said the sergeant as they were leaving. 'Had us all in fits with his stories.'

'Oh crikey,' said Dad. 'Did he tell you

the one about the dragon that lives under his bed?'

'No,' said the sergeant. 'But he told us he lived in a bus with a rainbow on top and rabbits and ducks round the outside. Fancy thinking up something like that!'

'Just fancy,' said Mum, and she giggled. She and Dad and the others were still laughing as they skipped off down the road back to the Rainbow Bus for a very late lunch.

5
The day they found the very best place ever

Three days in the seaside town were really quite enough, even for Tivvy, who bought so many pop posters and stickers she was beginning to run out of pocket money.

'It's so noisy,' said Mum. 'And it seems to go on all night.'

Dad and Uncle Billy were not much happier. They went fishing on the pier but it was so crowded they could hardly find a space. Dave and Andy tried playing football on the beach, but no matter where they went, the ball always seemed to land in the middle of someone's picnic. In the end a huge black dog joined in and when at last they got the ball back from him it was full of little holes.

'Never mind,' said Mum. 'You can always borrow Todger's ball.'

'It's got blue ducks all over it!' wailed Dave. 'You can't play *football* with a soppy thing like that.'

Three days were really quite enough.

'Maybe we should just pack up and move on,' said Mum. 'A Magical Mystery Tour. Let's just follow our noses.'

Next morning, though, it looked as if the seaside had packed up and gone. The sky was cold and grey and rainy. The deck-chairs flapped wet and soggy on the sea front, and the sand was empty except for a few people walking their dogs. Even the seagulls sat hunched and shivering with their backs to the wind. Andy knelt on the back seat and watched as the bus rolled off slowly past the shops.

'There's the place where I got my hat,' he shouted, waving to the lady who stood in the doorway staring out at the rain. She waved back.

'And there's where I got lost,' yelled Todger.

'Don't remind me,' groaned Mum. A policeman directing traffic turned and stared as the Rainbow Bus passed him. Then he spotted Todger and waved.

'You could cause a nasty accident doing

that,' laughed Dad, waving back.

Before long, they had left the town far behind and by teatime they had found a caravan park beside a long sandy beach. On the headland above the park stood a tall white lighthouse.

'You'll be able to read in bed tonight, anyway,' said Uncle Billy, parking the bus. But the park was almost as noisy as the seaside town. Children and dogs chased each other around the caravans and in the evening thumping music came from a Disco in the little hall by the camp shop.

Uncle Billy took Tivvy and Dave over to the hall while Mum tucked Todger and Rosie into bed and Andy went for a walk with Dad.

The sun was setting and the sky was beginning to darken as they came back to the bus. Andy stood on the cold sand staring up at the lighthouse as the huge silver light turned slowly, sending a brilliant beam out to sea.

'It's telling the big ships to stay away,' said Dad. 'There're too many rocks around here and I think it's beginning to get foggy too.'

He was right. An hour later, the

lighthouse was sounding its foghorn. *Wooooo-ooooo!* it wailed into the mist, again and again.

'I can't sleep,' wailed Todger, joining in from upstairs.

'If this goes on all night,' said Mum, 'I shall go quite *nuts!*'

Next morning the foghorn was quiet and the mist had cleared, but Mum insisted on leaving the caravan park and nobody argued with her.

The Rainbow Bus was bowling along the high road again, with everyone singing at the tops of their voices, when Uncle Billy suddenly put on the brakes and stopped.

'What's the matter? What's happened?' said Mum and Dad.

'Are we there?' said Andy, popping up to look out. Uncle Billy shook his head.

'We've got trouble,' he said, pointing to a trickle of white steam drifting up from the engine of the bus. 'The radiator's leaking. We'll have to keep filling it up with water until we can find a garage.'

They let the engine cool down and then filled the radiator again using the kettle and teapot. Uncle Billy started up and they drove off slowly down the road, leaving a long trickle of wet blobs behind them. On and on they went, but there was still no sign of a garage, and the water in the tank in the bus was beginning to run low.

'Got to keep enough to make a cup of tea,' said Mum. 'Let's find a river where we can stop for lunch.' By the middle of the afternoon they had run out of water again.

'Look,' said Dad. 'There's a trough in that cow field over there. I don't suppose they'll mind if we pinch some.' The cows stopped chewing as they pulled up and looked at the bus curiously.

Uncle Billy climbed over the fence with the kettle and teapot. Mum and Dad followed with the pots and pans from the bus. Andy climbed up, looked at the huge cows with their long curling horns, and decided to stay where he was by the bus.

'Oi, what are you lot up to?' came a yell from down the road and a little round man in blue dungarees, looking quite as fierce as the cows, came hurrying up.

'This here's private property, you know,' he puffed. His face was as red and shining as a tomato and his red hair stood up in little wild tufts around his head. Tivvy giggled and vanished into the bus. Dad pushed his way back through the cows and explained about the radiator.

'Well, I'm jiggered,' said the man. 'And so's your bus, too, by the look of it. But don't worry, my cousin Bob's garage is only a mile or two down the road. He'll soon have you right as ninepence.'

'We're looking for somewhere we can stop for the night, too,' said Mum.

'In the village,' said the man. 'It's just about right for your lot I'd say.' He winked at Andy and Dave.

'I suppose it'll have to do,' sighed Mum, as they drove on to the village. The garage was on the main road at the top of the hill. Below it a jumble of little grey stone houses wound down to a small harbour and the shining sea at the bottom.

'Take me a while to fix this lot,' said Bob, shaking his head over the engine. 'Why not take the kids down to the beach?'

Nobody needed to be told twice. They marched in a noisy, laughing procession down the main street. Everywhere curtains flapped in the breeze and each differently coloured front door stood wide

open in the afternoon sun. A fat, fluffy, orange cat lay like a hearthrug outside the Post Office and General Store, watching. Two old ladies stopped knitting and smiled as they passed.

'I like this,' said Dad, leaning on the harbour wall. Three or four small yachts bobbed gently in the clear green water. Beside them lay an old, fat, wooden boat that looked as if it had been painted with the odds and ends from all the front doors in the village.

'Sampies!' yelled Todger and grabbing Mum's hand, he dragged her off across a wide open grassy space to the beach. Dave and Tivvy raced ahead.

'Look at the rocks!' shouted Tivvy. 'I bet there's some great pools to explore.' Todger was already digging as if he had to shift the whole beach by teatime. Andy looked around. There were only a few other families on the sand, plenty of space to play football, and no big black dogs.

'Tide's coming in,' panted Dave, racing back up and peeling off his tee-shirt. 'I'm going swimming.' Andy sat down and started to pull off his shoes. The sand felt warm and tickly between his toes.

'What do you think?' said Mum, smiling up at him as she stretched out on the rug. 'Like it?'

'It's the very best place ever!' he yelled, racing down to join Dave and Tivvy. 'The very very best!'

6
The day Andy found some friends

'I'm fed up,' said Andy.

'Can't be,' said Mum. 'It's against the rules on holiday.' She smiled at him over the top of her sunglasses and went on reading. Andy lifted a handful of dry sand and let it trickle slowly through his fingers.

'Don't do that,' said Mum, shaking her book. 'It gets everywhere.'

Rosie was sitting on a corner of the rug, chewing the handle of Andy's plastic spade.

'That's mine,' he said, grabbing it. Rosie began to cry. Mum sighed and without putting down her book, reached a hand into her bag, pulled out Rosie's plastic duck and held it out. Rosie smiled, grabbed the duck and chewed its tail.

'Got nobody to play with,' said Andy, burrowing his fingers and toes into the sand. 'Tivvy and Dave won't let me go with them.'

'Play with Todger then,' said Mum. Down on the wet sand by the water's edge, Todger was piling sand into his bucket. He turned it upside down, bashed the bottom with his spade and lifted the bucket very carefully, leaving a very wobbly little sandcastle. He smiled, stood up, stamped the castle flat and started all over again. There was a whole row of little flattened lumps along the beach behind him.

'He's nuts,' said Andy.

'He's just the same as you used to be,' said Mum, turning a page.

'Wasn't,' said Andy. 'I haven't got any hands and feet.' His wrists and ankles disappeared down into the sand.

'Was so,' said Mum, putting down her book at last. 'I suppose no feet means we can't walk up to the village for an ice-cream?' Andy jumped up, scattering sand everywhere.

'Very clever!' said Mum, brushing it out of her hair. She picked up Rosie, called to Todger and they all walked up to the café.

But it was still a problem. Most of the

time Andy didn't have anyone to play with. When Dad suggested at teatime that Dave and Tivvy could take Andy with them, they both groaned.

'Do we have to?' moaned Tivvy. 'I've met some girls from the village and we don't want him tagging along. He only wants to play daft games!'

Uncle Billy and I are taking Dave fishing tomorrow,' said Dad. 'We'll be out in the boat all day, do you want to come?'

Andy shook his head. He didn't know what he wanted to do – he just wanted someone to do it with.

That night Mum tucked him into his sleeping bag and pulled the curtains in the tiny bus bedroom. Outside across the sea the sunset sky was fading from soft pink to pale blue.

'Look,' said Mum. 'You can just see the first stars. Quick, wish a wish.' Andy knelt on the bed beside her and watched the tiny gold stars sparkle low in the sky. They put their fingertips together, the way they always did and whispered the words.

'Star light, star bright,
First star I see tonight,'

I wish I may, I wish I might,
Have the wish I wish tonight.'

'Now,' Mum said. 'Wish hard!' Andy
screwed up his eyes and wished.

'It doesn't really work though, does it?'
he said as he snuggled down again. 'Dave
says it's just baby.'

'You never know,' said Mum. 'You
never know.'

Andy woke up next morning to an awful
lot of noise. Tivvy was bouncing around
making a fuss about her missing hairbrush
and calling down the stairs.

'Where do you think they came from?
Are they going to stay long?'

'How should I know,' Dad called up.
'Come and get your breakfast.'

'What's up?' said Andy, crawling out of
his sleeping bag.

'There's *hundreds* of people come,' said
Dave, clattering past him. 'And we've
been up for *hours* watching them.' Andy
pulled on his shorts and tee-shirt and followed the others downstairs. Then he
stopped and stared.

Across the green, on the other side away
from the cottages, were eight or nine huge,

square, grey trucks. Alongside them stood four large caravans with lace curtains at the windows, and two or three cars.

Men were unloading one of the vans and had lifted out some brightly painted wooden horses that lay on the grass kicking their legs in the air. Other painted pieces of wood lay around and the men seemed to be building a roundabout. Two children ran about laughing and chasing a shaggy brown dog.

The cornflakes sat uneaten on the table while everyone stared from the bus windows.

'Come and sit down,' said Mum. 'And don't be so rude. I expect if they wanted to put on a show they'd sell tickets!'

'I suppose they will,' said Uncle Billy. 'Looks like a Fairground.' The brown dog bounced across to the Rainbow Bus with the children racing him. He picked up something and started to shake it.

'That's my bucket,' yelled Andy, tumbling out of the door. He came face to face with the two children who were standing staring up at the bus. Side by side they looked exactly the same, with curly black hair and round brown faces.

'That your bus?' said the boy. Andy nodded.

'What happened to it?' giggled the girl.

'Nothing,' said Andy. 'We live in it. Don't we, Mum?'

"Course we do,' said Mum. 'Are you two twins?' They nodded.

'But I'm older,' said the girl.

'Only five minutes,' said the boy, poking her.

'Like some cornflakes?' said Mum. In no time at all the twins were sitting up at the table on either side of Andy, munching cornflakes and talking non-stop.

'I'm Angela Veronica Mary,' said the girl. 'And he's Kevin William.'

'Kev,' said the boy, munching quietly. 'And everyone calls her Angie.'

'Do you live in a caravan?' asked Tivvy.

'Most of the time,' said Angie. 'Sometimes we stay with our Gran. She's got a house. But mostly we travel round with the Fair.'

'Imagine living on a Fairground!' said Andy.

'We've done it for years and years,' said Kev.

'Seven and three quarter years,' said Angie. 'We'll be eight in September.'

'Me too!' said Andy, bouncing about with excitement. 'I'm eight at the end of September.'

'Our birthday's in the middle,' said Angie grandly. 'So we're older than you.'

'But you can come and play with us,' said Kev.

Andy didn't need a second invitation. He spent all morning with Angie and Kev. He sat on the grass with them and watched as their Dad and the other men put up the roundabouts. There were small cars and horses and a tiny fat red fire engine with a shining gold bell.

'That's our ride,' said Angie. 'My Mum and Dad's. You can help rig it if you like. Can't he, Dad?'

'Looks like a handy lad to have around,' said the twins' Dad. 'Welcome aboard, sir.'

So Andy helped the others to lift the pieces of wood and hand them to the men as they asked for them. In no time at all, the little cars and motorbikes and the fat red fire engine were fastened down and the roundabout was ready to use. They stopped for a mug of tea and some biscuits, and then went on to put up stalls and sideshows and a striped tent for the twins' Aunt Rena who was a Fortune Teller.

They carried a chair and a small round table into the little sunlit tent, that smelt of fresh grass. Andy sat on the chair and watched as Angie spread a soft red cover on the table. In the middle she put a

cushion, and on the cushion was a shining, clear, glass ball.

'Does she really know what's going to happen?' said Andy, peering at the ball. All he could see was his own face upside down, fat and curving.

'Well, she told our Dad his car was going to break down,' said Angie. 'And it did.'

'The man in the garage said that weeks ago!' said Kev. 'It's an *ancient* car.'

The Fairground was wonderful, and Andy was so excited he could hardly stop for soup and sandwiches at lunchtime.

'Do you want to come with us this afternoon?' said Tivvy. 'We're having a game of rounders with some of the kids from the village. You can play in my team if you promise not to drop the ball.'

'I've got work to do,' said Andy, finishing the last of his sandwich and milk. 'Haven't got time to play silly games.'

That night, as they walked back across the green from the Fair, Mum turned and looked back. The cars and the fat little fire engine spun round and round like a musical box under the coloured lights. Jingly music mingling with the warm smell of hot dogs, toffee apples and candy floss followed them into the dark around the bus.

'Did you enjoy that?' said Mum. She was carrying Todger who had fallen fast asleep. Andy was skipping along behind, clutching two white plaster dogs with red collars that he and Dad had won at one of the stalls.

'Scurrrrumptious!' he sang, twirling round and round on the grass to the roundabout music.

That night he took his plastic bucket up to the bedroom, turned it upside down by his bed and sat the dogs on it.

'I'll call them Angela Veronica Mary and Kevin William,' he whispered as Mum tucked him in.

'Good idea,' she giggled, pulling the curtains. 'Look, there are more stars out tonight.' Out over the sea where the sky was dark blue, tiny pale sparks of gold twinkled like the Fairground lights.

Suddenly Andy sat up in bed. 'My wish came true,' he said. 'It really did.'

'Aha,' said Mum. 'Told you it would. Perhaps Aunt Rena was working some magic on it too. Goodnight, sleep tight.'

She tiptoed off downstairs and Andy fell asleep with the faint sound of the music from the Fairground dancing round and round in his head.

7
The day they had tea with the ghost

It was Mum's Castle-Visiting Day.

'This one's glorious,' she said, waving a book from the Tourist Office. 'It's got battlements, a moat and a drawbridge – and the Earl still lives in it. You'll love it – there's even a ghost.'

Tivvy and Dave pulled a face. Mum was daft about castles. Once she got in, it was always very difficult getting her back out again. They had all spent hours wandering round old ruins looking for her.

This one was no ruin though, they had to admit, it was really good.

'It's just like the castle in the toy shop window last Christmas,' said Andy. A square grey stone tower rose out of the dark trees. Tiny windows glittered in the afternoon sun and a bright yellow and red flag fluttered above the battlements.

'It looks like a Sleeping Beauty castle,' said Tivvy, as they climbed out of the Rainbow Bus.

'More like a spooky one,' said Dave. 'Bet we see the ghost. Bet you're too scared to come in with us, Andy.'

'Am not!' yelled Andy, watching as Dad and Uncle Billy took Todger and Rosie off to feed the ducks on the lake. 'Wait for me.'

His feet made a strange hollow noise as he ran across the wooden drawbridge to catch up with Mum and the others. Together they walked through the stone archway into a dark and shadowy courtyard. Above the arch, two tiny black windows peered down like watching eyes.

'Murder holes,' said Mum, her voice echoing off the high walls. 'They used to pour all sorts of horrible things down on to people trying to break in.'

'School dinner soup,' said Dave with a gruesome chuckle, as Mum led the way into the castle. Andy shivered, giggled and hurried on after her.

Inside, the castle was a maze of corridors linked by twisting stone staircases. In one room the walls were hung with dark shiny paintings of people in strange clothes. From one huge gold frame, a man stared down with bright black eyes. He had the sort of face that looked as if he knew a secret but was keeping it to himself.

'He's the one that's supposed to be the ghost,' whispered Tivvy, creeping up behind Andy. He hurried on very quickly and bumped into Mum, who had stopped at the door of a small bedroom. Most of the space was filled by a huge four-poster bed draped with tattered pink curtains and covered with a faded pink bedspread. There was an enormous carved bed-head with fat wooden gold-painted angels staring down at the pillow.

'Imagine trying to read in bed with that lot watching you!' Mum laughed.

'There's some slippers underneath,' said Andy, kneeling on the carpet and squinting sideways. 'Do you think the Earl still sleeps in here?'

'Wouldn't surprise me at all,' said Mum. 'It's a funny old castle this is.'

It went on being a funny old castle. In one room a huge, ugly, black cabinet stood on four fat wooden legs with claws. It looked as if it was just about to get up and

walk out.

'Horrible,' said Mum, then she laughed again as she read the label. 'This dreadful 19th century monstrosity hides an even more dreadful one – a 20th century television set.'

It was like that everywhere. Large serious pieces of furniture and gloomy paintings had funny little notices beside them. In the dining room an old gentleman with a badge saying GUIDE turned and smiled as they stared at the huge table set with shining silver plates.

'I wonder what it was like to eat off those,' said Tivvy, imagining herself as a princess.

'Noisy,' said the old gentleman. 'All that clattering of knives and forks. Couldn't hear yourself think!'

'Just like home,' sighed Mum, moving on.

At the top of another twisting stone stair, a large black cardboard arrow pointed down. It read: TO THE DUNGEON.

'It's gha-a-a-a-a-stly,' Dave's voice floated back up to them. 'Come on, hurry up!' He gave a wicked chuckle. Andy stopped.

It looked very dark down there and at the bottom a black iron gate stood half open.

'It's all right,' said Mum quietly. 'He's only kidding. Do you want to hold my hand?' Andy shook his head. He would have taken Mum's hand but Tivvy was watching. He followed very closely behind them as they went down.

It was much colder in the dungeon and very gloomy. The walls felt damp as Andy reached out a hand to steady himself on the stairs. No sun shone in through the tiny slits of windows high in the wall and the only light came from a small glass case full of old keys and pieces of rusty chain. Andy edged closer to Mum and held on to the handle of her bag. They stood in the middle of the floor and waited as Dave and Tivvy explored the dark corners.

'Time to go,' said Mum at last, looking at her watch. Dave and Tivvy raced on ahead to find Dad, and Andy stayed with Mum. She pulled the iron gate shut then stopped half-way up the stairs to read another notice on the wall. Andy looked back down into the dungeon. It was dark and empty and didn't seem quite so spooky somehow, looking through the gate. He tiptoed down to the bottom step.

'Halloooooooo,' he whispered. 'Anybody there . . .'

Suddenly he froze. Clank, clank, clank! Silence.

Tap, tap, tap and then the clanking again. Something metal scraped across the stone floor. But there was no-one there!

Andy opened his mouth to yell for Mum. Crash, clatter came the noise again. Something crawled out of a low archway in the darkest corner and stood up, shaking itself in a cloud of dust.

'Fiddlesticks!' muttered the Something. 'Have to get the plumber in again.'

It was the elderly gentleman from the dining room.

'Hello,' he said, looking up and chuckling at Andy's face. 'Gave you a bit of a shock did I?' Andy nodded.

'You didn't think I was the ghost, did you?' he chuckled. Andy nodded again. The man roared with laughter and the sound echoed round the dungeon.

'Sorry to disappoint you,' he said. 'I'm only his great, great, great grandson and

I'm having trouble with the central
heating.' He stopped brushing himself
down and looked at Andy.

'Don't suppose *you're* a plumber,' he
said. Andy smiled and shook his head.

'My brother Billy could help,' said Mum.
In no time at all, Uncle Billy was down in

the dungeon with his jacket off, clanking and banging away like a first-class ghost.

'Should charge the visitors extra today,' said the man. 'They don't usually get the spooky noises during the day.' Andy stared up at him.

'Is there really a ghost then?' he squeaked.

'Only at night,' the man whispered. 'Most inconsiderate when you're trying to watch telly.' The clanking settled to a gurgle and a soft humming noise as Uncle Billy crawled out of the corner brushing himself down.

'Splendid!' said the elderly gentleman. 'Good for another five hundred years, I'm sure. Now, you must all come and have tea with me once the visitors have gone. Nothing posh, it's the housekeeper's night off.'

They had sandwiches, scones, jam and fruit cake in a big, bright kitchen at the back of the castle.

'That reminds me,' said the elderly gentleman, watching Andy spreading raspberry jam, 'of what happened when they cut off the third Earl's head . . .' It was like that all the way through tea – he told the most gruesome funny stories.

'Revolting!' said Mum, pouring another cup of tea, but she laughed and listened like everyone else.

When they had finished and cleared away the tea things, the elderly gentleman took a torch and led them back through the darkened castle to the front gate. Andy stayed close beside him, watching everywhere for some sign of the ghost, but everything was quiet and peaceful.

'He doesn't seem to be about,' said the elderly gentleman. 'I'm sorry.'

'Maybe he's having a night off,' said Andy. 'Like the housekeeper.'

The elderly gentleman was still laughing as he came out to the car park to wave goodbye and admire the Rainbow Bus.

'Sorry I frightened you earlier,' he said, pressing a tiny box into Andy's hand. 'You'll come back again, won't you?'

'Yes please,' shouted Andy and they all waved as the bus swung off down the road. Behind them the lights of the castle flickered and vanished among the trees. The others crowded round as Andy opened the little box.

'What's in it?' said Dave. Andy took out

something small and heavy, wrapped in soft white tissue paper.

'It's a ghost,' laughed Tivvy as he unwrapped it. But it wasn't.

It was an old toy soldier – a tiny knight in a suit of shining silver armour. In one hand he carried a sword, in the other a red and yellow shield. It was chipped and worn as though some small boy a long time ago had played and played with it.

Underneath it, in the box lay a card with the Earl's name and a crown printed on one side. On the other side he had written:

FOR ANDY,
FROM THE GHOST'S GREAT,
GREAT, GREAT GRANDSON.

8
The day of the Inside Outing

It was raining. For the first time since the night of the thunderstorm it was raining so hard that the beach, the sea and even the little village had all but vanished in the grey mist.

The Rainbow Bus sat all alone like Noah's Ark in a world that was running with water.

'I'm fed up,' grumbled Dave, drawing squiggles on the steamy windows. 'Can't go swimming.'

'You don't have to,' said Dad, pulling on his anorak to walk up to the village. 'Just stand outside for five minutes. Coming?'

Nobody wanted to go with him. They sat staring glumly out at the rain.

'Why don't you three big ones have a game of Snakes and Ladders?' suggested Mum. They tried that, and Ludo too, but

Tivvy kept winning. Dad came back to find them all arguing.

'It *is* my turn,' said Tivvy, thumping the table. 'Sure it is, Andy.'

''Tis not,' said Dave. 'Cheat, cheat, cheat. We're not going to play with you any more.' Andy didn't know whose side to be on.

'What are they playing?' said Dad, shaking himself dry.

'Happy Families,' sighed Mum. It went on like that until lunchtime, and Dad had had enough.

'What this Happy Family needs,' he said, 'is an outing.'

'Have you found another castle?' said Mum hopefully. Dad shook his head.

'A fairground!' said Andy.

'Don't be daft,' said Tivvy. 'It's still bucketing out there!'

'Doesn't matter,' said Dad. 'We're going on an Inside Outing.'

Once they were on the road everyone began to cheer up.

'Where are we going?' said Andy. 'What's an Inside Outing?'

'Aha,' said Dad. 'Just wait and see.'

The Inside Outing was a big, square,

yellow-painted building with a sign outside saying VISITORS CAR PARK. A man in a white coat and hat waved from a door at the end.

'Quick!' he shouted. 'Come inside.'

Mum grabbed Rosie and Dad carried Todger. Holding anoraks above their heads and running on tiptoe to avoid the puddles, they all raced across the car park to the door and tumbled in.

'Just in time,' said the man in the white coat. 'We're about to run the film, and then there's a Guided Tour.'

Andy looked around the room. There was a group of people sitting on small chairs in front of a big white screen. Some looked up and smiled as they came in. Round the walls hung posters and coloured photographs of fruit and vegetables. From a door on the other side of the screen they could hear a strange humming and clinking noise. Andy sniffed. There was a beautiful smell, sweet and warm. It reminded him of something but he couldn't think what.

'Mum . . .' he said.

'Shhhh,' said Mum. 'The film's starting. Sit down.' Andy felt around for a chair as the lights went out.

'That's my foot,' grumbled Tivvy.

'Playschool,' said Todger as the screen lit up, and Andy giggled. At last everyone was settled and the film began.

It wasn't a cartoon – it was really rather boring. The story seemed to be all about a lady who made jam and soup a long time ago and then started a little shop to sell them. The jam and soup were now made in a big new factory and there were pictures of all the farms and fields where the fruit and vegetables came from.

'Mooooo!' shouted Rosie, pointing at some cows. It was a new word she had learned since coming on holiday.

Andy fidgeted on the plastic chair. Most of the film was dull except when they showed the line of shining red jam jars going through the machine and coming out with their labels and tops stuck on. Or the silver soup tins clattering along one behind the other, queuing up to be filled.

At last the film came to an end, the man in the white coat switched on the lights and led them all through the door behind the screen.

'This way for a tour round the factory,' he said. Dad picked up Rosie and followed Tivvy, Dave and Uncle Billy. Andy got up to go and Todger stayed where he was.

'Come on,' said Mum. Todger held on to the seat.

'More Playschool,' he said firmly. 'Want to see the cartoon.'

'There isn't one, dope!' said Andy. 'It's not telly.' But Todger had made up his mind he was staying.

'You can't stop there,' said Mum. 'We've got to go with the others.' She started to walk towards the door. Todger began to cry.

'Well come with me,' said Mum. Todger shook his head and cried louder.

'Want Playschool,' he wailed, holding on to the chair tighter than ever. He howled as Andy tried to tip him off from behind.

'Andy, that's no help at all!' said Mum. 'Why don't you just go and find the others?' Andy left and went through the door behind the screen down a white corridor. Ahead of him he could hear the humming and clinking – behind him, Todger!

He turned a corner and stopped and stared. The delicious sweet smell was stronger than ever.

Through a row of big glass windows in the wall he was looking down into the factory. Beneath him heaps of shining red strawberries slid slowly along a table. Ladies in white coats and hats stood on either side, turning them over. Sometimes they picked out a strawberry and dropped it into a bucket underneath. At the end of the table was a huge, round, silver tub, bigger than a bath and full of something bubbling and steaming. It was a deep, rich red with patches of pink floating on the surface. Andy suddenly remembered Mum making strawberry jam last summer. That's what the smell was!

He looked around and saw Dad and the others staring through some windows on the other side of the room. They were watching a table covered in vegetables and another huge steaming bath. There was some shining silver machinery whirling and clonking in a corner. A radio was playing pop music and a young woman standing beside the jam tub was singing to herself and doing a little dance as she watched it bubble.

Andy went racing back to Mum and Todger, who was still sitting sniffing on the chair.

'Come on, come on!' he said. 'It's just like Playschool! There's a funny machine, and somebody dancing and all sorts of Through The Window things . . . just like telly.'

'You're kidding,' said Mum.

Todger stopped sniffing, climbed down off the chair, took Andy's hand and went with him.

'Well, really!' said Mum, following them.

They walked slowly round all the
windows, gazing down into the factory.
Todger stood, fascinated, as Andy pointed
out the jam tub and the machinery. The
young lady was still dancing and tapping

out a tune with a huge silver spoon on the side of the tub. Todger stood for ages, sniffing and hiccuping and watching the table where the vegetables were being cut up.

'What are they doing?' he said at last.

'Making soup,' said Mum. You could smell it cooking.

'I'm hungry,' said Todger, sniffing.

A lady who was chopping onions and sniffing smiled up at him and waved.

'They don't do that on Playschool,' said Andy. Todger laughed and ran on ahead to catch up with Dad and the others who were waiting for them.

Mum winked at Andy and took his hand. 'Clever old you,' she said.

Together they skipped out, across the rainy car park and into the Factory Shop to buy some tins of soup and a pot of shining strawberry jam for tea.

9
The day they went home

'The nice thing about holidays,' said Mum, 'is that they don't go on forever.'

'They wouldn't be holidays if they did,' said Dad, squashing the last of his pullovers into the big tartan bag and pulling the zipper shut before it popped out again. 'Who'd like a mug of cocoa?'

'Me!' said Mum and Uncle Billy and Tivvy and Dave and Andy and Todger all at once. Rosie waved her hands and gurgled as Mum fastened her into her sleeping suit – it looked as if she meant yes too.

'Why's it nice?' said Andy. 'I don't want to go home.'

'I do,' said Tivvy. 'I've got lots of new posters for my room and badges to swop.'

'I'm going to play for the school football team after the holidays,' said Dave. 'Old

Bouncy Griffiths said so.'

'I'll get back to the garden,' said Dad, handing round the mugs. 'The grass must be a bit shaggy by now.'

'Back to work,' sighed Uncle Billy. 'I can't wait!'

'Back to a cup of tea,' said Mum, lifting the big thick mug. 'First thing I'll do is have a cuppa from my best china tea set.'

'Don't want to go,' said Andy, looking out across the beach and the little village as Mum tucked him into bed. He stretched out in his own tiny room in the front of the bus and looked around. The seagull hat sat on top of his zipper bag, the plastic bucket was full of shells and pebbles. Angela Veronica Mary and Kevin William, the two china dogs he and Dad had won at the Fairground, sat beside it.

'Going home's fun too sometimes,' said Mum, tiptoeing back downstairs. 'Be good to get back to peace and quiet again.'

'No it's not – it's boring,' grumbled Andy, snuggling down for the last time.

But going home was quite different to what any of them had expected.

'Looks like they knew we were coming,' laughed Uncle Billy as he turned the corner into the High Street. The whole street was bright with flags and baskets of flowers hung from the lamp-posts.

'Look at the Cosy Kettle,' shouted Tivvy. The little tea shop was draped with pink and silver ribbons and a small tree in a tub on the pavement was smothered in pink and silver bows.

'The sports shop!' yelled Dave. The window was hung with a huge banner covered with coloured football rosettes. It looked as if they came from every team in the country.

'And dear old Blossom,' laughed Mum. Blossom was the model in the dress shop window. She was tall and spiky with frizzy plum-coloured hair and wore some very peculiar clothes. Today she had on a red velvet cape and a small silver and diamond crown perched like a bird in among the plum-coloured frizz. From one elegant finger hung a notice: MISS PAREE SAYS WELCOME TO THE GALA QUEEN.

'Gala Day!' said everyone at once.

'Fancy forgetting it was today,' said Mum as they all tumbled over in a heap on the cushions. Uncle Billy had put on the brakes rather suddenly. A tall policeman stood in the road in front of the Rainbow Bus holding back the traffic.

'You're going the wrong way, sir,' he called. 'It's over to the right.'

'But . . .' said Uncle Billy.

'If you hurry up you'll just catch the rest of them,' said the policeman.

'I don't want . . .' said Uncle Billy.

'Come along now, sir,' said the policeman rather sharply. 'We're holding up the rest of the traffic.'

Uncle Billy shrugged and turned off to the right down a side street.

'Hurry up,' yelled a man with a ticket pinned on his jacket. 'They're just leaving now.' He waved Uncle Billy round a corner.

'Where are we going?' said Andy. Suddenly they stopped. The bus had pulled into a supermarket car park behind a long line of decorated vans and lorries. Crowds of people stood by the side of the road watching as the biggest lorry, covered with pink and silver ribbons like the Cosy Kettle, pulled out.

'Oooh look!' yelled Tivvy. 'It's the Gala Queen. She's the girl from the tea room.'

The lorry bounced into the High Street with the Gala Queen sitting high on a gold-painted chair. She was a tall, slim girl, rather like Blossom, although her hair was blonde instead of plum-coloured. She waved with one hand and held on to her silver crown with the other. All around her chair stood other girls in white dresses, holding on and smiling and waving. They were followed by two other lorries loaded with people in fancy dress costumes.

There were clowns, pirates, cowboys and spacemen.

'Milk van,' shouted Todger. And there, sure enough, was the little milk float that came round each morning. The top was covered in leaves and flowers. In the back, instead of piles of plastic crates, there was a covering that looked like grass and three bears sat round a picnic basket. They munched sandwiches and waved to the crowd. Todger waved back.

'Your turn next!' shouted a man waving to Uncle Billy and the Rainbow Bus.

'But we're not ...' said Uncle Billy. Nobody heard a word he said as a lorry drove past with a brass band playing on the back.

'Come on,' laughed Dad. 'Just go!' Uncle Billy swung the Rainbow Bus out into the High Street behind the brass band.

'Seventy Six Trombones ...' blared the trumpets. Uncle Billy tooted along with the music and joined the Big Parade.

The crowds along the High Street waved and cheered. A clown on a bicycle banged on the side of the bus and waved up at them. Todger bounced back from the window. Andy laughed, stuck his nose flat against the glass and made a face. The clown wobbled, stuck his tongue out and pedalled on to catch up with the band.

All the way down the High Street the crowds laughed and waved and danced around the Parade. The sun sparkled on the Rainbow Bus, the shining trumpets of the brass band and all the flags and ribbons.

The Gala Queen smiled and smiled as the long line of lorries turned into the park opposite the Town Hall.

There were tents with sideshows, a disco, sports and all sorts of stalls. They

parked the Rainbow Bus in the middle and piled out to join in the fun.

There, standing waiting for them, was a little old man with a crinkly brown face, white curly hair and a big toothless smile.

'I thought it was my bus,' chuckled George. 'Can't be two painted like that! She looked real pretty in that parade. Best of the lot if you ask me.'

For the rest of the afternoon they had a wonderful time. Tivvy spent the very last of her pocket money on a tee-shirt with her favourite pop-singer on the front. All round his head was a ring of pink glittering stars. Dad bought Todger a teddy bear mask from one of the stalls and a pink and silver balloon to float above Rosie's carrycot. They all jumped about and cheered as Dave galloped to first place in one of the races and came back with a huge red rosette and a very small silver cup.

'You can always use it for your breakfast egg,' said Mum.

Andy, wearing his seaside seagull hat wandered round the Gala with George and Uncle Billy, looking at lorries, vans and some very old steam rollers and traction engines that sat in a corner puffing and smoking.

At the end of the long, noisy afternoon they all met up back at the Rainbow Bus for soup and hot dogs as the car park emptied around them.

Mum looked around the table at Tivvy in her starry, pop tee-shirt, Dave with his enormous red rosette, Andy's funny seagull hat and Todger's teddy bear mask smiling back at her. Rosie slept happily in her carrycot.

'And to think I was looking forward to coming back to peace and quiet,' she laughed. 'Did you all enjoy yourselves?'

'YES!' they all shouted with a great happy roar as Uncle Billy started the engine to drive back down the brightly lit High Street.

'*The wheels on the bus are going home . . .*' sang Andy, bouncing up and down on the cushions.

They were all still singing, Andy loudest of all, as they slowly bumped to a halt outside their very own garden gate.